Ready For Reading!

LEVEL 2

D0279479

Dear Parents,

Congratulations! Your child has embarked on an exciting journey – they're learning to read! As a parent, you can be there to support and cheer them along as they take their first steps.

At school, children are taught how to decode words and arrange these building blocks of language into sentences and wonderful stories.

At home, parents play a vital part in reinforcing these new-found skills. You can help your child practise their reading by providing well-written, engaging stories, which you can enjoy together.

This series offers exactly that, and more. These stories support inexperienced readers by:

- gradually introducing new vocabulary
- using repetition to consolidate learning
- gradually increasing sentence length and word count
- providing texts that boost a young reader's confidence.

As each book is completed, engaging activities encourage young readers to look back at the story, while a Picture Dictionary reinforces new vocabulary. Enjoyment is the key – and reading together can be great fun for both parent and child!

Prue Goodwin
Lecturer in Literacy and Children's Books

# How to use this series

This series has 4 levels. The facing page shows what you can expect to find in the books at each level.

As your child's confidence grows, they can progress to books from the higher levels. These will keep them engaged and encourage new reading skills.

The levels are only meant as guides; together, you and your child can pick the book that will be just right.

Here are some handy tips for helping children who are ready for reading!

 Give them choice – Letting children pick a book (from the level that's right for them) makes them feel involved.

 Talk about it – Discussing the story and the pictures helps children engage with the book.

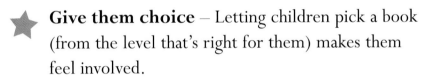 **Read it again** – Repetition of favourite stories reinforces learning.

 Cheer them on! – Praise and encouragement builds a child's confidence and the belief in their growing ability.

LEVEL **1** For first readers

* short, straightforward sentences
* basic, fun vocabulary
* simple, easy-to-follow stories of up to 100 words
* large print and easy-to-read design

LEVEL **2** For developing readers

* longer sentences
* simple vocabulary, introducing new words
* longer stories of up to 200 words
* bold design, to capture readers' interest

LEVEL **3** For more confident readers

* longer sentences with varied structure
* wider vocabulary
* high-interest stories of up to 300 words
* smaller print for experienced readers

LEVEL For able readers

* longer sentences with complex structure
* rich, exciting vocabulary
* complex stories of up to 400 words
* emphasis on text more than illustrations

Once you have read the story, you will find some amazing activities at the back of the book! There are Excellent Exercises for you to complete, plus a super Picture Dictionary.

But first it is time for the story . . .

Ready?

Steady?

Let's read!

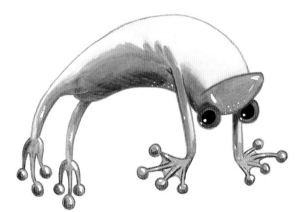

Michael Catchpool   David Roberts

Hopping Mad!

Little Tiger
LONDON

Fred had
five frogs.

So did Finn.

One night, Finn's frogs called
to Fred's frogs, "Come and
have a party!"

So Fred's frogs hopped over
the fence.

The frogs had a
fantastic time.

When the sun came up,
they hopped back
over the fence.

The next morning,
Fred counted his frogs.
There was one missing.

Fred was furious.

Fred snatched back
his frog.

Then he built his fence higher.

That evening, Fred's frogs
called to Finn's frogs,
"Come over to our pond!"

The frogs had great fun. Then Finn's frogs squeezed back under the fence.

The next day, Finn counted his frogs. Two were missing!

Finn was fuming. He snatched back his frogs.

Then he dug a big ditch by
the fence.

That evening, Finn's frogs
called to Fred's frogs, "Fancy
another party?"

They all had a splendid time.
Then Fred's frogs leaped back
over the ditch and scrambled
over the fence.

The following morning,
Fred counted his frogs.
He was missing three!

Fred was frantic.

He snatched back his frogs.
Then he built a cage over
his pond.

Later, Finn's frogs freed
Fred's frogs.

Now Fred and Finn have
no frogs.

But Fiona – who lives next door – has TEN!

Croak! Croak! Croak!

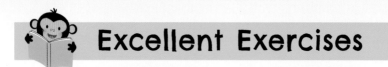
Have you read the story? Well done!
Now it is time for more fun!

Here are some questions about the story. Ask an adult to listen to your answers, and help if you get stuck.

Perfect Pets

This story is about two boys who have lots of pet frogs. If *you* could have any pet, what would it be?

Party Animals

Can you count all the frogs in this picture? What do *you* like to do at parties?

Sad Frogs

Now describe what Fred is doing in this picture.

Finally Free

Can you remember where the frogs go at the end?

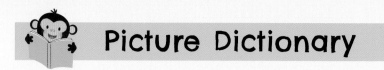

Picture Dictionary

Can you read all of these words from the story?

cage

counted

ditch

dug

fence

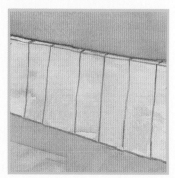

frog

fun

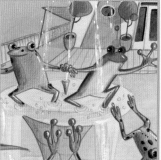

furious

hopped

pond

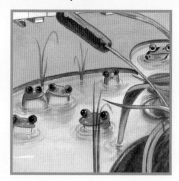

Can you think of any other words that describe these pictures – for example, what colours can you see? Why not try to spell some of these words? Ask an adult to help!

Newton

Newton keeps hearing funny noises! "Don't be scared!" he tells his toys. And he sets off in the dark to find out what is making the scary sounds.

Ouch!

Hedgehog is about to go to sleep when OUCH! an apple lands on her back! Will her friends be able to help her?

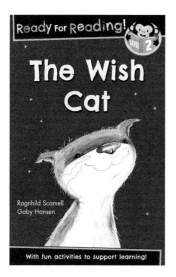

The Wish Cat

Holly wants a cute little kitten more than anything else in the world. But when she wishes on a star, she ends up with a scruffy cat instead!

Where There's a Bear, There's Trouble!

Where there's a bee there's honey. So when Bear spies a bee, he chases after it. But, where there's a bear, there's trouble. So the bee buzzes off as fast as it can . . . !

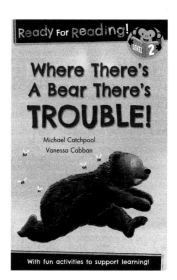

In memory of my dad — M C
For Lynn and Oberon — D R

LITTLE TIGER PRESS LTD,
an imprint of the Little Tiger Group
1 The Coda Centre, 189 Munster Road, London SW6 6AW
First published in Great Britain 2004
This edition published 2017
Text copyright © Michael Catchpool 2004, 2013
Illustrations copyright © David Roberts 2004, 2013
All rights reserved
Printed in China
978-1-84869-738-6
LTP/1800/1856/0417
2 4 6 8 10 9 7 5 3 1

More books from Little Tiger Press!

LEVEL 1 – For first readers

Can't You Sleep, Dotty?

Fred

My Turn!

Rosie's Special Surprise

What Bear Likes Best!

LEVEL 2 – For developing readers

Hopping Mad!

Newton

Ouch!

Where There's a Bear, There's Trouble!

The Wish Cat

LEVEL 3 – For more confident readers

Lazy Ozzie

Little Mouse and the Big Red Apple

Nobody Laughs at a Lion!

Ridiculous!

Who's Been Eating My Porridge?

LEVEL 4 – For able readers

The Biggest Baddest Wolf

Meggie Moon

Mouse, Mole and the Falling Star

The Nutty Nut Chase

Robot Dog